Mrudul Tata

THE MONKEY AND THE CROCODILE

AND OTHER STORIES

Retold by: **MRUDUL TATA**
Illustrated by: **HOLLEY BENTON**

TATA PUBLISHING

For
Samir *and* **Sanjiv**
My Constant Sources of Inspiration

First Impression 1995.

Printed in Hong Kong.

Library of Congress Catalog Card Number 94-90319

ISBN 0-9639913-2-9

INTRODUCTION

Long ago there lived an Indian King who had three sons. The princes were very dull and lazy. Many teachers were tried but the princes were unable to learn anything. Then one day a learned old man undertook the task of teaching them. He told them stories of birds and animals which the princes listened to very attentively and from the stories learned the art of living a life where friendship, trust and respect play a very important role. This collection of ancient stories originally written in Sanskrit is known as "The Panchatantra." Three of the most popular stories are retold in this book.

Dedicated to Ganesh, Lord of Wisdom

CONTENTS

THE MONKEY AND THE CROCODILE

O nce upon a time a monkey lived on a beautiful rose apple tree by the bank of a wide river. He spent most of his day swinging from branch to branch and playing with the wild birds. Whenever he got hungry, he ate the delicious rose apples that grew on the tree.

One day, a crocodile searching for food swam up to the bank of the river and came to rest under the tree. The monkey saw the crocodile through the branches and, full of curiosity, carefully came down. Perching at a safe distance from the crocodile he asked, "Who are you? Where did you come from?"

The crocodile, not having eaten for days, was very weak. In a feeble voice he replied, "I am a crocodile from the other end of the river. I have wandered here looking for food."

The monkey, being very kind at heart, said, "Do you like rose apples? They are very tasty. Here, take some!" He then picked some of the rose apples from the tree and threw them down. The crocodile ate the rose apples, enjoying every crunchy bite. The monkey and the crocodile soon became good friends.

Early one morning, they decided to explore different places along the river. The monkey swung from branch to branch and the crocodile followed him through the water. As they went around a bend in the river, they came to a lovely spot where the river narrowed and turned into a swamp. They liked the swamp and decided to spend some time there.

As they were chatting together one afternoon, the crocodile told the monkey that he lived with his beautiful wife at the other end of the river.

"I wish you had told me this earlier," said the monkey. "I would have given some of the delicious rose apples for your wife. Please take some for her tonight!"

The crocodile took the rose apples and thanked the monkey. He quickly swam home and gave the rose apples to his wife. She enjoyed eating them and begged her husband to get some more. The crocodile promised her that he would do so. He adored his wife and could never deny her anything. From then on, the crocodile would always bring rose apples home to his wife that the generous monkey gave. His wife loved eating the rose apples, but was jealous that her husband spent so much time with the monkey.

One sweltering afternoon, as the crocodile's wife floated lazily in the water, she muttered to herself, "If the rose apples are so sweet, then the monkey who eats them must be even sweeter."

When her husband returned home that evening, she pretended to be very sick. The crocodile got worried and asked her, "My dear, are you ill? Is there something I can get to make you feel better?"

"Oh," moaned his wife, "only a monkey's heart can cure me."

"What!" cried the crocodile in horror, not believing his ears. "A monkey's heart?"

"Yes," whispered his wife. "If you love me and want me to get well, you will have to get me a monkey's heart."

"I cannot do it," pleaded the crocodile. "The monkey is my friend and has always been nice to me. He trusts me. I cannot deceive him."

"Well," sighed his wife, "then I will have to die!"

The crocodile loved his wife dearly and did not want anything to happen to her. So he thought and thought, and finally decided to bring the monkey home.

At dawn the next day, as the rays of the sun lifted the early morning mist, the crocodile swam up to the rose apple tree. He politely requested the monkey to visit their home. The monkey readily accepted the invitation. Carrying as many rose apples as he could for his friend's wife, he hopped on to the crocodile's back.

The crocodile swam swiftly and silently with the monkey on his back. When he reached the deepest part of the river, he started to dive under the water. The monkey, trembling with fear, cried out to the crocodile, "Please, my friend, do not go any further! I cannot swim! I shall drown if you take me any deeper!"

"That is exactly what I want to happen," replied the crocodile.

"But why?" asked the frightened monkey in disbelief. "What have I done that you want to kill me? I am your friend and have always helped you."

"Well," answered the crocodile, "my wife is sick and only a monkey's heart will cure her."

Shocked at the crocodile's treachery, the monkey was greatly hurt. He knew he was in grave danger.

Staying calm the monkey shrewdly said, "Is that all? Why did you not let me know this before? I always keep my heart in the branches of the rose apple tree so that it is safe. If you had told me earlier, I would have brought it with me. Let us go back and fetch my heart so that your wife can have it."

The crocodile, without thinking, started swimming back to the bank of the river. As soon as they returned, the monkey leaped off the crocodile's back and quickly scampered up the rose apple tree. Safe at last, he sat high on the tree and scornfully said to the crocodile, "Now go tell your wife that she cannot have my heart since she is married to a fool!"

The crocodile knew that he had been outwitted by the clever monkey. He swam away, never to return.

THE DONKEY AND THE JACKAL

O nce upon a time a donkey lived with his master, a poor washerman, in a small village by a winding river. Everyday the donkey would carry a huge load of clothes for his master to the river. There the washerman cleaned the clothes, dried them in the sun, and folded them into a pile. By evening, they returned to the village with the clean load of clothes on the donkey's back. After a hard day's work, the washerman would let the donkey wander freely in the village.

One evening, as the donkey was walking on the outskirts of the village, he met a scrawny jackal and they started talking. The jackal and donkey soon became very good friends. They would meet every evening and go in search of food.

Wandering around late one night, the donkey and the jackal found themselves on the other side of the village. In the moonlight they saw beautiful fields with all kinds of delicious vegetables. Feeling very hungry, the two friends went into a field and ate as many vegetables as they could.

From then on, they went to the field every night. After eating what they liked, they talked for a while, and then went home. Soon the donkey and the jackal grew strong and healthy.

As they were eating turnips in the field one night, the donkey said to the jackal, "My dear friend, the night is very beautiful and quiet. The lovely full moon and bright stars in the sky inspire me to sing."

Alarmed at his friend's idea, the jackal pleaded, "Please do not sing. Your voice in the still of the night will wake up the farmer."

"Do not worry," said the donkey, "he will not hear me. He lives at the other end of the field."

"Remember," warned the jackal, "we have been eating the farmer's vegetables every day. He will be furious if he finds us."

"In any case, I must sing," replied the stubborn donkey. "I feel absolutely happy."

"Well," said the jackal, "since you will not see reason, I will wait outside the field. I am certain you will get into trouble."

Soon the donkey started braying, thinking he was singing in the most melodious voice. The farmer heard the braying and immediately knew it was the donkey who had been eating the vegetables at night.

He jumped out of his bed, fetched a heavy stick, and ran into the field to catch him. He found the donkey near the turnip patch and started beating him.

The donkey was so lost in his singing that he did not notice the angry farmer until he was hit by the stick. Although he ran as fast as he could, he was no match for the farmer.

Eventually the donkey managed to escape, but not until the farmer had given him a good thrashing. He dragged himself out of the field to meet his friend, the jackal, who was waiting anxiously for him.

With a pained look the donkey said to the jackal, "You were so right. Singing for my supper was not such a good idea after all!"

THE HUNTER AND THE GEESE

A flock of wild geese lived on a large sprawling tree deep in a jungle. Every day they left the tree at dawn in search of food and returned at dusk. Of all the geese, the oldest one was the wisest. As he was resting one day, he noticed a small creeper at the foot of the tree. Knowing that it would get strong as it wound its way up, he felt the creeper would pose a danger to the flock.

"My friends, we must get rid of this creeper," he warned. "It is easy to destroy now, while it is still small and weak." But the rest of the geese did not heed him. "The creeper is only a harmless weed," they scoffed.

As the days went by, the creeper grew strong. It wound around the tree like a thick rope. One spring evening, a hunter passing by in search of food saw the flock of geese land on the tree.

"If I catch these geese, I will not have to hunt for days," thought the hunter. "I shall come back tomorrow and lay a net to trap them."

The next morning when the geese flew away in search of food, the hunter climbed up the tree with the help of the creeper. He carefully spread his net on the branches of the tree.

At dusk the geese returned but did not see the net in the dark. As soon as they perched on the branches, they were trapped. All night they tried in vain to free themselves. "What shall we do?" cried all the geese desperately.

"Well," said the oldest bird just before dawn, " if we do not act fast, we will be dead by morning. There is only one way to escape and that is to pretend to be dead. When the hunter comes tomorrow, he will believe that all of us are dead and will start throwing us down. As soon as the last one hits the ground, we must fly away at once. But remember, we do not move until every one is on the ground."

Early the next morning, the hunter found the flock of geese lying dead in his net. He started throwing all the birds down one by one. Visions of a wonderful feast were already dancing in his head. But when the last goose hit the ground, the whole flock suddenly flew away.

Surprised by the cleverness of the geese, the hunter walked away empty handed.